Dragolin

Written by: Stephen Cosgrove
Illustrated by: Robin James

A Serendipity™ Book

PRICE STERN SLOAN
Los Angeles

Dedicated to Susan Lowe, the Wedgewood School and a city called Baton Rouge. A person, a place and a time where what I wrote was reflected in other's eyes.
Stephen

Once, in a place and time far, far away, where magical things grow in great profusion, were the swamps and marshes of Weezalana. They were not your ordinary swamps and marshes, but rather a magical place with magnolia trees above and Spanish moss below. It was a place of long-legged birds and lazy rivers that lulled the land to sleep with their melodic ripples lapping at the shore.

Weezalana was a bit of land here and a bit of land there, connected by graceful arched bridges of flowering willow trees.

In the land of Weezalana lived creatures beyond your imagination. Flying horses with great spreading wings who nested high in the magnolia trees, centaurs who gamboled about the tiny areas of meadow—and, of course, the dragons. Great and monstrous dragons lolled about the edges of the swamp, dipping their toes in the warm, sluggish waters of the river. They were scaled beasts with large amber eyes who cared for nothing and occasionally blew blasts of smoke and flame into the air just to brighten up the sky.

Strange creatures all, but none was stranger than a short, plump little dragon named Dragolin. Now it was true that Dragolin, the same as all the dragons, had scales like flakes of emerald-green stone. And it was true that he had beautiful, sad amber eyes. But what he didn't have, what made him strangest of all, for a dragon, was that he couldn't flame a flame or even puff a cloud of smoke.

Oh, he would try! He would scrunch up his face into the most amazing contortion and grunt and groan—but the best he could do was blow a bit of half-baked smoke out his nose. The other dragons left Dragolin all alone. They didn't want to be cruel, and watching that pudgy little monster try to light his flame was funny beyond words.

One day, as Dragolin was trying with all his might to bake a small pathetic beetle with no result, an armadillo happened by. He was just waddling by, the way most armadillos do, when he noticed this most unferocious dragon turning blue just by trying to burn a bug. Armadillos normally have no sense of humor whatsoever, but the sight of this dragon with his eyes bulging out was more than the little armadillo could take. He leapt high into the air, then rolled onto his back, giggling and tickling himself into the mud.

Poor Dragolin was so humiliated that large, oily tears began to roll down his snout, drowning whatever chance he had of building a fire.

With a bit of effort the armadillo was able to stop his laughing, and after wiping the tears of joy from his eye he asked, "For why do you cry, little dragon?"

Dragolin, having nothing better to do and in great need of baring his soul, told the armadillo his whole story. He told him of the humiliation and shame of not being able to light the ceremonial fires of Dragon Days farther down in the swamp. He told the little creature how all of his fears had been realized when no flame, not even a little spark, would leap from his mouth as it was supposed to. And worse than that, ". . . until I can light the ceremonial flame the other dragons won't even think of me as a fellow dragon." With that, Dragolin burst once again into tears.

"Look," said the armadillo, "if you'll stop crying I'll tell you the very simple secret of the swamps of Weezalana and you shall have all the flame you desire." Instantly Dragolin's tiny ears perked up and he stifled his tears with a choke and a sob.

"The secret," the armadillo continued, "is very, very simple: If you believe . . . there is nothing that you can't do!"

Dragolin hiccoughed and said in a small voice, "Just believe? That's all I have to do?"

"Yuup!" replied the armadillo, satisfied that he had solved the problem. "Just believe with all your might and there is nothing you can't do." With that he waddled on his way.

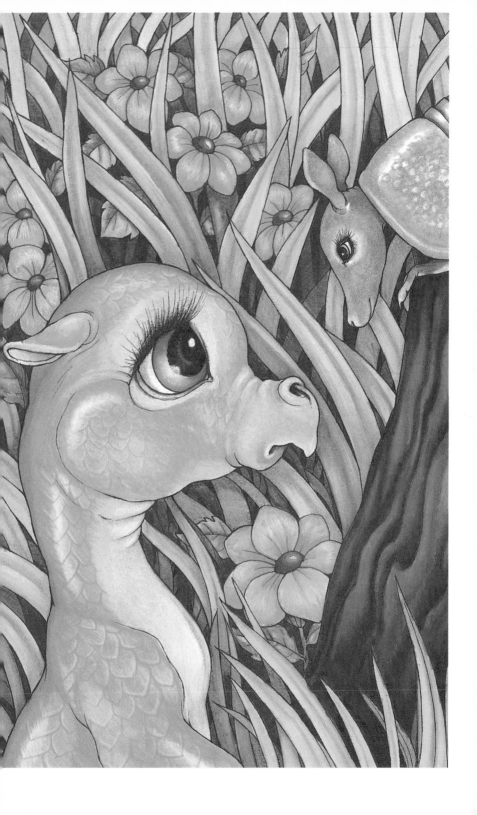

"Just believe, huh?" Dragolin muttered to himself.

Just then one of the great flying horses swooped low over the trees as if it were testing a swirl of wind. Dragolin's eyes opened wide in wonder. "Then I believe that I can fly!" His face contorted with the effort of believing, he climbed high into the branches of a great magnolia tree.

His eyes scrunched closed in deep concentration, Dragolin took a deep, heavy breath and soared off the branch in a great glide. Unfortunately, that great glide only lasted the length of a very short sneeze, and Dragolin smashed into the mud, far below.

With much effort he pulled himself from the mud and goo and then sat on the bank reflecting on what had happened. "I did everything the armadillo said. I really believed I could fly! But maybe I just didn't believe enough." So the poor, pathetic dragon sat in the shade of the tree, thinking.

"I guess I've just got to believe harder," he thought as he sat there with furrowed brow.

He sat there, thinking, hours and hours. Finally the armadillo happened by again and noticed the little dragon sitting in rigid concentration. The armadillo watched for a while without being noticed and then asked, "Ahem! What are you doing?"

"Why," Dragolin said, a bit perturbed at being disturbed, "I'm concentrating on believing. As you said, 'If you believe, there's nothing you can't do!' The first time I tried, I didn't believe enough. This time I'm going to really believe." Once again he closed his eyes tightly and went back to concentrating.

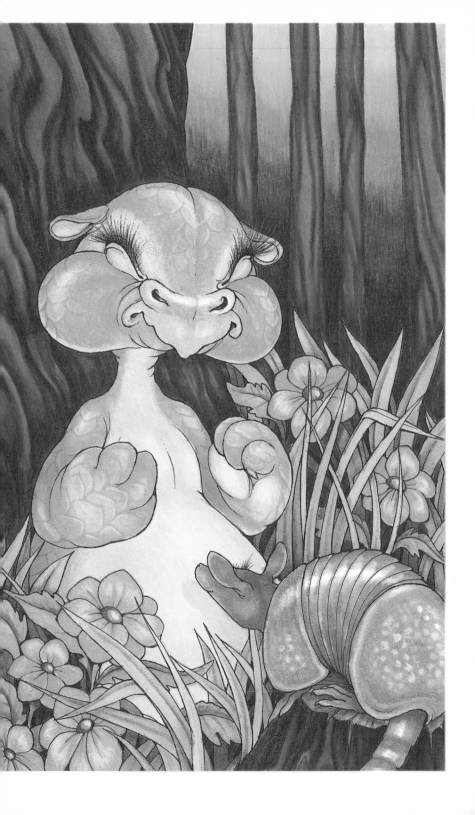

After some time Dragolin began to mutter, over and over, "I can, I can! I do believe and I know I can!"

"Believe you can what?" asked the armadillo, who had stayed to watch, fascinated by the little dragon's antics.

"I believe," said Dragolin, dragging himself up on his webbed feet, "that I can . . . walk through that tree!"

Before the armadillo could stop him, the dumb little dragon walked right into the tree. But the tree must have believed more than he. First, Dragolin's snout, then his body, smashed into the tree and the best he could do was get a large bump on the head for his efforts.

The armadillo held back his laughter as he helped the silly dragon to the edge of the river. With some water-soaked moss he wiped the tears from Dragolin's face. "Listen, little dragon," he said consolingly, "you can do anything, anything at all, if you believe, but first you have to believe you can do something your body is capable of doing. You could believe that you could swim, and with a lot of practice and a lot of believing I'm sure you could swim! But if you were a rock, no matter how much you believed you could swim, you still would sink if you threw yourself in the water."

Dragolin stared at his new-found friend. "You mean," he sputtered, "that if I believe I can make fire and flame come from my mouth and if I'm physically able . . . then I will make dragon's fire?"

The armadillo smiled and said, "Now you understand. All you have to do is believe with all your might and nothing is impossible!"

From that day forward Dragolin made flame and dragons' fire whenever he wished because he believed. Sometimes on cold, blustery days he would warm himself and his friend the armadillo by turning some moss and twigs into a cheery fire.

So as you stand there wishing
On a far and distant star,
Remember: by believing,
You can be better than you are.

Serendipity™ Books

Written by Stephen Cosgrove
Illustrated by Robin James

Enjoy all the delightful books in the Serendipity Series:

The above books, and many others, can be bought wherever books are sold, or may be ordered directly from the publisher.

PRICE STERN SLOAN

360 North La Cienega Boulevard, Los Angeles, California 90048